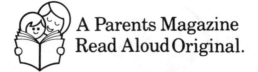

A Parents Magazine
Read Aloud Original.

Library of Congress Cataloging in Publication Data
Wiseman, Bernard.
   Cats! Cats! Cats!
   Summary: Miss Kittikat brings home so many cats that
soon they must all find a new place to live.
   [1. Cats—Fiction]   I. Title.
PZ7.W7802Cat   1984   [E]   83-27288
ISBN 0-8193-1127-8

CATS! CATS! CATS!

by B. Wiseman

Parents Magazine Press ~ New York

For my gang
and Stephanie

10 9 8 7 6 5 4 3

Miss Kittikat was a lady
who loved cats.
One day she found a kitten
who had no home.
He looked tired and hungry.
"Come with me," she said.
"I will take good care of you!"

This was not the first cat
Miss Kittikat had taken home.

When she opened the door,
fifteen other cats meowed, "Hello!"

The cats were hungry,
so Miss Kittikat gave
each one a bowl of food.
It was hard work feeding so many cats.
But Miss Kittikat did not mind.

Then she put a pillow in a box
for the new kitten.
"This will be your bed," she said.
"Sleep well."

The kitten was not the last cat

Miss Kittikat brought home.

Soon there was no room for
the cats to sleep.
Miss Kittikat called Mr. Hardhammer.
"Can you help?"

Mr. Hardhammer loved cats, too.
So he built bunk beds for them.

But the bunk beds were not enough.

So Mr. Hardhammer put up tents
and made treehouses.

But they were soon filled up, too.
"I must stop bringing home cats,"
said Miss Kittikat.
"There is no more room."

The next day, Miss Kittikat walked
right past two hungry kittens.

But when she heard their meows,
she ran back to get them.

On the way home,
Miss Kittikat had an idea.
"Can you build more rooms *on top*
of my house, Mr. Hardhammer?"
"Of course I can!" he said.

Mr. Hardhammer called in
Mr. Bangnails, Mrs. Saw-Wood,
and Mr. Drillscrew to help.

They made the tallest house
on the block.

But there still was not enough room for all those cats.

"We cannot build more rooms,"
said Mr. Hardhammer.
"But there is a big ship
on the river that no one uses."

"You and your cats
can live there!" he said.
So they moved the cats to the ship.

But when Miss Kittikat started

filling up the ship...

it sank lower and

lower in the water.

"There is another place we can try,"
said Mr. Hardhammer.
"It is an old train
just outside of town."

So they moved onto the train.
Every time they needed room,
they added a car.

But one day,
they ran out of tracks!

"What will we do now?"
cried Miss Kittikat.

Mr. Hardhammer had one more idea.
He and his crew went right to work

with wood and tools,
brushes and paints.

"Come and see what we've done!"
said Mr. Hardhammer the next day.
All along the roads were signs that said:

CATS! CATS! CATS!
Give a cat a happy home!

People came from far and wide.

They all promised
to give the cats happy homes.

Miss Kittikat moved back into her house

with fifteen cats and one kitten.

Miss Kitticat still brings home cats.
But now there is a home for every one.

About the Author

BERNARD WISEMAN was a *New Yorker* cartoonist/idea man for many years. He left cartooning to start a series of stories for children that was syndicated in Sunday papers nationwide, and then turned to creating children's books.

While working on CATS! CATS! CATS!, Mr. Wiseman sometimes had visitors to his studio. Looking at the pictures, many of them said they wished they could take one of the cats home. Which cat would *you* choose?